AIR FRYER

RECIPES FOR BEGINNERS

Publications International, Ltd.

Art on front cover and page 1 © Shutterstock.com.

Pictured on the front cover *(left to right):* Chocolate-Peanut Butter Dessert Wontons *(page 180),* Green Bean Fries *(page 42)* and Buffalo Cauliflower Bites *(page 50).*

Pictured on the back cover *(clockwise from top left):* Garlic Air-Fried Fries *(page 150),* Air-Fried Beef Taquitos *(page 82),* Mini Spinach Frittatas *(page 12),* Loaded Tater Tots *(page 30)* and Bang Bang Chicken *(page 60).*

ISBN: 978-1-63938-238-5

Manufactured in China.

8 7 6 5 4 3 2 1

Microwave Cooking: Microwave ovens vary in wattage. Use the cooking times as guidelines and check for doneness before adding more time.

WARNING: Food preparation, baking and cooking involve inherent dangers: misuse of electric products, sharp electric tools, boiling water, hot stoves, allergic reactions, food borne illnesses and the like, pose numerous potential risks. Publications International, Ltd. (PIL) assumes no responsibility or liability for any damages you may experience as a result of following recipes, instructions, tips or advice in this publication.

While we hope this publication helps you find new ways to eat delicious foods, you may not always achieve the results desired due to variations in ingredients, cooking temperatures, typos, errors, omissions, or individual cooking abilities.

Let's get social!

 @Publications_International

@PublicationsInternational

www.pilbooks.com

TABLE OF CONTENTS

INTRODUCTION

It seems like everyone is air frying these days—with good reason! The air fryer not only makes delicious, crispy, crunchy—and often healthier—food, but it also makes everyday cooking quicker and easier.

Learn the basics of air frying with more than 90 super simple recipes for any time of day, from breakfast to dessert and everything in between. You may have thought that your air fryer only prepares healthier "fried foods," but you'll find that you can prepare a wide variety of dishes including appetizers, snacks, sandwiches, vegetables and so much more. Mini frittatas and homemade bagels are two of the impressive but easy air-fried breakfasts. Chicken wings and tortilla chips are crowd pleasers you can make with minimal time and mess. Or cook sensational steak, chicken and pork chop dinners in no time—it's all easier with an air fryer!

HELPFUL TIPS

- Read the manufacturer's directions for your air fryer carefully before cooking to make sure you understand the specific settings and features of your machine.

- Preheat your air fryer for 2 to 3 minutes before cooking.

- To avoid foods sticking to your air fryer basket, use nonstick cooking spray or cook on parchment paper or foil. Spraying food occasionally with nonstick cooking spray during the cooking process will also help food to brown and crisp more easily.

- Don't overfill your basket. Smaller air fryers may require cooking food in several batches. Some foods should be cooked in a single layer for best results (as noted in the recipes), so cook these items in batches as needed. Crowding the basket will prevent foods from crisping and browning evenly.

- Use toothpicks to hold food in place. Sometimes light foods may blow around from the pressure of the fan, such as the top of a quesadilla or the top slice of bread in a sandwich. Securing foods in the basket with toothpicks can prevent this from happening.

- Check foods during cooking and turn the food or shake the basket for even browning, if necessary. This will not affect cooking times—once you return the basket, the cooking (and the timing) resumes.

- Experiment with cooking times of various foods, as different models of air fryers may cook slightly faster and cooking times can vary. Test foods for doneness before serving them; check meats and poultry with a meat thermometer, and use a toothpick to test muffins and cupcakes.

- Use a foil sling to get cake pans or baking dishes in and out of the air fryer basket. Fold a 24-inch piece of foil into a 2-inch-wide strip; place the pan in the center and use the ends to hold and raise or lower the dish into the air fryer. Tuck the ends down while cooking so the drawer can close.

- You can use your air fryer to cook foods typically prepared in the oven. But because the air fryer is more condensed than a regular oven, it is recommended that you reduce the temperature by 25°F to 50°F and reduce the cooking time by 20 percent when converting standard oven recipes to the air fryer.

- Use your air fryer to cook frozen foods, too! Frozen French fries, fish sticks, chicken nuggets, individual pizzas—these all work wonderfully in the air fryer. Just remember to reduce the cooking temperatures and times as recommended above.

ESTIMATED COOKING TEMPERATURES/TIMES*

FOOD	TEMPERATURE	TIMING
Beef (ground beef)	370°F	15 to 17 min.
Beef (steaks)	390°F	10 to 15 min.
Chicken (bone-in)	370°F	20 to 25 min.
Chicken (boneless)	370°F	12 to 15 min.
Fish	390°F	10 to 12 min.
Frozen Foods	390°F	10 to 15 min.
Pork	370°F	12 to 15 min.
Vegetables (asparagus, broccoli, corn on the cob, green beans, mushrooms, tomatoes)	390°F	6 to 10 min.
Vegetables (bell peppers, cauliflower, eggplant, onions, potatoes, zucchini)	390°F	10 to 15 min.

This is just a guide. All food varies in size, weight, and texture, so be sure to test your food for doneness before consuming it. For best results, some foods will need to be shaken or turned during cooking.

BREAKFAST & BRUNCH

HOMEMADE AIR-FRIED BAGELS

makes 4 servings

1 cup self-rising flour
1 cup plain Greek yogurt
1 egg, beaten

Sesame seeds, poppy seeds, dried onion flakes, everything bagel seasoning (optional)

1. Combine flour and yogurt in bowl of stand mixer.* Mix with dough hook at medium-low speed 2 minutes or until well blended. Continue to mix 4 to 5 minutes or until dough is smooth and elastic.

2. Shape dough into a ball. Cut dough into four pieces; roll each piece into a ball. Pull and stretch dough to create round bagel shape, inserting finger into center to create hole.

3. Preheat air fryer to 330°F. Line basket with parchment paper. Place bagels on parchment paper; brush with egg and sprinkle with desired toppings.

4. Cook bagels 8 to 10 minutes or until lightly browned. Serve warm.

Or, use heavy spatula to mix dough in large bowl. Turn out onto lightly floured surface; knead 4 to 5 minutes or until dough is smooth and elastic.

AIR-FRIED OMELET SCRAMBLE

makes 2 servings

2 eggs
2 tablespoons milk
¼ teaspoon salt
⅛ teaspoon black pepper
2 tablespoons chopped red
  and/or green bell pepper

2 tablespoons chopped onion
4 tablespoons (1 ounce) shredded
  Cheddar cheese, divided

1. Spray 6×3-inch baking dish* or two small ramekins with nonstick cooking spray.

2. Preheat air fryer to 350°F.

3. Whisk eggs, milk, salt and black pepper in medium bowl until well blended. Stir in bell pepper, onion and 2 tablespoons cheese. Pour into prepared baking dish.

4. Cook 10 to 12 minutes or just until eggs are set but still wet, breaking up eggs slightly after 5 minutes. Top with remaining cheese.

Depending on the size of your air fryer, you may need to modify the size of the baking dish.

QUICK CHOCOLATE CHIP STICKY BUNS

makes 12 sticky buns

1 package (about 11 ounces) refrigerated French bread dough

¼ cup sugar

1 teaspoon ground cinnamon

½ cup mini semisweet chocolate chips

⅓ cup chopped pecans, toasted*

2 tablespoons butter, melted

1 tablespoon maple syrup

To toast nuts, cook in preheated 325°F parchment paper-lined air fryer 3 to 4 minutes or until golden brown.

1. Unroll dough on lightly floured cutting board or work surface. Combine sugar and cinnamon in small bowl; sprinkle evenly over dough. Top with chocolate chips.

2. Starting with short side, roll up dough jelly-roll style. Cut crosswise into 12 (¾-inch) slices with serrated knife.

3. Combine pecans, butter and maple syrup in 9-inch round cake pan;* mix well. Spread in even layer. Arrange dough slices cut sides up in pan, pressing gently into pecan mixture.

4. Preheat air fryer to 370°F.

5. Cook buns 8 to 10 minutes or until golden brown. Invert onto serving plate; scrape any pecans or butter mixture remaining in pan over buns. Serve warm.

If 9-inch pan will not fit in your air fryer, use smaller baking dish and cook sticky buns in two batches.

MINI SPINACH FRITTATAS

makes 6 mini frittatas

6 eggs
2 tablespoons milk
¾ cup thawed frozen chopped
  spinach, squeezed dry
¼ cup shredded white Cheddar
  cheese

¼ cup grated Parmesan cheese
1 teaspoon dried minced onion
½ teaspoon salt
⅛ teaspoon black pepper
  Dash ground red pepper
  Dash ground nutmeg

1. Preheat air fryer to 330°F. Spray six 4-ounce ramekins* with nonstick cooking spray.

2. Whisk eggs and milk in large bowl. Stir in spinach, Cheddar, Parmesan, dried onion, salt, black pepper, red pepper and nutmeg until blended. Divide mixture evenly among ramekins.

3. Cook frittatas 12 minutes or until eggs are puffed and firm and no longer shiny. (Cook in batches if necessary.) Cool 5 minutes.

4. Loosen bottom and sides with small spatula or knife; remove to wire rack. Serve warm or at room temperature.

*Or use a 6-cup standard muffin pan if this fits in your air fryer. Spray with nonstick muffin spray.

BISCUIT DOUGHNUTS

makes 8 doughnuts

1 package (about 16 ounces) refrigerated jumbo biscuits (8 biscuits)

¼ cup honey
1 teaspoon chopped pistachio nuts

1. Separate biscuits. Poke hole in center of each biscuit with hands or handle of wooden spoon to create doughnut shape.

2. Preheat air fryer to 370°F.

3. Cook doughnuts in batches 7 to 8 minutes or until golden brown.

4. Drizzle warm doughnuts with honey; sprinkle with pistachios. Serve immediately.

VARIATION: For cinnamon-sugar coating, combine ¼ cup sugar and 1 teaspoon ground cinnamon in small bowl. Roll warm doughnuts in cinnamon-sugar to coat.

OMELET CROISSANTS

makes 2 servings

2 large croissants
2 eggs
¼ cup chopped mushrooms
¼ tablespoon chopped red and/or
    green bell pepper

¼ teaspoon salt
    Pinch black pepper
¼ cup (1 ounce) shredded
    Cheddar cheese

1. Cut lengthwise slit across top of each croissant. Use hands to break open croissants and pull apart slightly to create space for eggs.

2. Whisk eggs in medium bowl; stir in mushrooms, bell pepper, salt and black pepper. Spoon mixture into croissant openings; sprinkle with cheese.

3. Preheat air fryer to 330°F. Line basket with parchment paper.

4. Cook croissants 12 to 15 minutes or until eggs are set and croissants are lightly browned.

CRESCENT SAUSAGE WRAPS >>

makes 6 servings

1 package (8 ounces) refrigerated
   crescent dough sheet
1 package (about 12 ounces) fully
   cooked breakfast sausage links

Maple syrup (optional)

1. Unroll dough on cutting board or work surface; cut into thin strips. Wrap each sausage link with dough. Insert wooden skewers* through sausages.

2. Preheat air fryer to 370°F.

3. Cook skewers 5 to 7 minutes or until dough is golden brown. Cool slightly; serve with maple syrup for dipping.

Soak wooden skewers in water 20 minutes to prevent burning. Depending on the size of your air fryer, you may need to trim the skewers to fit.

FRENCH TOAST STICKS

makes 4 servings

4 eggs
⅓ cup milk
1 teaspoon ground cinnamon
1 teaspoon vanilla

4 slices Italian bread, cut
   into 3 pieces each
Powdered sugar
Maple syrup

1. Whisk eggs, milk, cinnamon and vanilla in large shallow dish until well blended.

2. Dip bread pieces in egg mixture, turning to coat.

3. Preheat air fryer to 370°F. Line basket with parchment paper; spray with nonstick cooking spray.

4. Cook bread in batches 8 to 10 minutes or until golden brown. Sprinkle lightly with powdered sugar; serve with maple syrup.

MINI BROCCOLI FRITTATAS

makes 4 mini frittatas

1 small broccoli crown
  (about 4 ounces)
1 tablespoon olive oil
¼ cup chopped red onion
2 tablespoons water
½ teaspoon salt, divided
2 tablespoons chopped roasted
  red pepper

Pinch red pepper flakes
¼ cup crumbled goat or feta cheese
4 eggs
2 tablespoons grated Parmesan
  or Asiago cheese
2 tablespoons chopped fresh basil
  or ½ teaspoon dried basil
¼ teaspoon black pepper

1. Peel off tough outer skin of broccoli stem with paring knife; chop stem into ¼-inch pieces. Chop top of broccoli into small florets (about ½ inch).

2. Heat oil in large skillet over medium-high heat. Add onion; cook and stir 2 minutes. Add broccoli, 2 tablespoons water and ¼ teaspoon salt; cook and stir about 5 minutes or until broccoli is crisp-tender. Add roasted pepper and red pepper flakes; cook and stir 1 minute. Transfer vegetables to small bowl; stir in goat cheese.

3. Preheat air fryer to 330°F. Spray four 4-ounce ramekins with nonstick cooking spray. Divide vegetable mixture evenly among prepared ramekins.

4. Whisk eggs, Parmesan, basil, remaining ¼ teaspoon salt and black pepper in medium bowl until well blended. Pour egg mixture over vegetables in ramekins.

5. Cook 15 to 18 minutes or until toothpick inserted into centers comes out clean. Cool 5 minutes. Serve in ramekins or run small knife or spatula around edges to loosen and turn out onto plates.

BREAKFAST FLATS

makes 4 servings

1 package (about 14 ounces) refrigerated pizza dough
1½ cups (6 ounces) shredded Cheddar cheese

8 slices bacon, crisp-cooked and crumbled (optional)
4 eggs, fried or scrambled
Coarse salt and black pepper

1. Unroll dough on work surface; divide into four pieces. Shape each piece into 6×4-inch oval. Place dough on parchment paper; top with cheese and bacon, if desired.

2. Preheat air fryer to 370°F.

3. Place flatbreads with parchment paper in basket; cook in batches 4 to 6 minutes or until crusts are golden brown and cheese is melted.

4. Top with fried eggs; season with salt and pepper. Serve warm.

QUICK JELLY–FILLED DOUGHNUT BITES

makes 20 doughnut balls

1 package (about 7 ounces)
  refrigerated biscuits
  (10 biscuits)
¼ cup coarse sugar

1 cup strawberry preserves*

*If preserves are very chunky, process
in food processor 10 seconds or press
through fine-mesh sieve.*

1. Separate biscuits. Cut each biscuit in half; roll dough into balls to create 20 balls.

2. Preheat air fryer to 370°F. Place sugar in large bowl.

3. Cook doughnuts in batches 5 to 6 minutes or until golden brown. Roll warm doughnuts in sugar to coat.

4. Fill piping bag with medium star tip with preserves. Poke hole in side of each doughnut with paring knife; fill with preserves. Serve immediately.

CRUSTLESS SPINACH QUICHE

makes 6 servings

8 eggs
1 cup half-and-half
1 teaspoon Italian seasoning
¾ teaspoon salt
½ teaspoon black pepper

1 package (10 ounces) frozen chopped spinach, thawed and squeezed dry
1¼ cups (5 ounces) shredded Italian cheese blend

1 Preheat air fryer to 330°F. Line 8-inch round baking pan* with parchment paper; spray with nonstick cooking spray.

2 Whisk eggs, half-and-half, Italian seasoning, salt and pepper in medium bowl until well blended. Stir in spinach and cheese; mix well. Pour into prepared pan.

3 Cook 30 minutes or until toothpick inserted into center comes out clean. Cover with foil if top is browning too much. Remove to wire rack; cool 10 minutes.

4 To remove quiche from pan, run knife around edge of pan to loosen. Invert quiche onto plate and remove parchment paper; invert again onto serving plate. Cut into wedges.

*If 8-inch pan doesn't fit in your air fryer, use two smaller baking pans and cook in batches, reducing cooking time slightly.

APPETIZERS & SNACKS

AIR–FRIED BOWTIE BITES

makes 8 to 10 servings

8 ounces uncooked bowtie (farfalle) pasta or favorite shaped pasta (such as shells or tubes)
1½ tablespoons olive oil
¼ cup grated Parmesan cheese

½ teaspoon salt
½ teaspoon garlic powder
¼ teaspoon black pepper
   Marinara sauce, warmed (optional)

1 Prepare pasta according to package directions until al dente. Drain pasta (do not rinse); transfer to large bowl.

2 Preheat air fryer to 390°F.

3 Drizzle pasta with oil. Add cheese, salt, garlic powder and pepper; toss to coat.

4 Cook pasta in single layer 10 to 12 minutes or until lightly browned and crisp around edges, shaking occasionally during cooking. (Cook in batches if necessary.) Season with additional salt and pepper; serve with marinara sauce, if desired.

LOADED TATER TOTS

makes 3 to 4 servings

1 package (16 ounces) frozen bite-size potato nuggets (tater tots)

½ cup (2 ounces) shredded Cheddar cheese

2 slices bacon, crisp-cooked and crumbled* or 2 tablespoons bacon bits

2 tablespoons sour cream

2 green onions, chopped
Chopped avocado (optional)

Cook bacon in preheated 390°F air fryer 6 to 8 minutes or until crisp. Remove to paper towel-lined plate; cool completely.

1. Preheat air fryer to 390°F.

2. Cook potatoes in single layer 6 to 8 minutes, shaking occasionally during cooking. (Cook in batches if necessary.)

3. Transfer potatoes to baking dish that fits inside air fryer; sprinkle with cheese and bacon. Cook 2 to 3 minutes or until cheese is melted.

4. Drizzle with sour cream; sprinkle with green onions and avocado, if desired. Serve immediately.

BUFFALO WINGS

makes 4 servings

1 cup hot pepper sauce
1/3 cup vegetable oil, plus additional
    for brushing
1 teaspoon sugar
1/2 teaspoon ground red pepper
1/2 teaspoon garlic powder

1/2 teaspoon Worcestershire sauce
1/8 teaspoon black pepper
1 pound chicken wings, tips
    removed, split at joints
Blue cheese or ranch dressing
Celery sticks (optional)

1. Combine hot pepper sauce, 1/3 cup oil, sugar, red pepper, garlic powder, Worcestershire sauce and black pepper in small saucepan; cook over medium heat 20 minutes. Remove from heat; pour sauce into large bowl.

2. Preheat air fryer to 370°F. Brush wings lightly with additional oil.

3. Cook wings in batches 16 to 18 minutes or until golden brown and cooked through, shaking halfway through cooking.

4. Transfer wings to bowl of sauce; stir to coat. Serve with blue cheese dressing and celery sticks, if desired.

MOZZARELLA STICKS

makes 12 servings

¼ cup all-purpose flour
2 eggs
1 tablespoon water
1 cup plain dry bread crumbs
2 teaspoons Italian seasoning
½ teaspoon salt

½ teaspoon garlic powder
1 package (12 ounces) string
  cheese (12 sticks)
Marinara or pizza sauce, warmed

1. Place flour in shallow dish. Whisk eggs and water in another shallow dish. Combine bread crumbs, Italian seasoning, salt and garlic powder in third shallow dish.

2. Coat each piece of cheese with flour. Dip in egg mixture, letting excess drip back into dish. Roll in bread crumb mixture to coat. Dip again in egg mixture and roll again in bread crumb mixture. Place on baking sheet. Refrigerate until ready to cook.

3. Preheat air fryer to 370°F. Line basket with parchment paper; spray with nonstick cooking spray.

4. Cook mozzarella sticks in batches 8 to 10 minutes or until golden brown, turning halfway through cooking. Serve with marinara sauce.

GARLIC ROASTED OLIVES AND TOMATOES

makes about 2 cups

1 cup assorted olives, pitted
1 cup grape tomatoes, halved
4 cloves garlic, thinly sliced

1 tablespoon olive oil
1 tablespoon herbes de Provence

1. Pat olives dry with paper towels.

2. Combine olives, tomatoes, garlic, oil and herbes de Provence in medium bowl; mix well.

3. Preheat air fryer to 370°F.

4. Cook olive mixture 5 to 7 minutes or until tomatoes are browned and blistered, shaking occasionally during cooking. Transfer to serving bowl.

SERVING SUGGESTION: Serve with toasted bread slices for an appetizer or toss with hot cooked pasta for a main dish.

PITA CHEESE STRAWS

makes 6 servings

3 (6-inch) pita bread rounds
    or naan breads
2 tablespoons butter, melted
1 clove garlic, minced

1 teaspoon Italian seasoning
¼ cup grated Parmesan cheese
½ teaspoon salt
   French onion dip (optional)

1. Split pitas in half horizontally. Combine butter, garlic and Italian seasoning in small bowl; mix well.

2. Brush tops of pitas with butter mixture; sprinkle with cheese and salt. Cut into ½-inch strips with pizza cutter or kitchen scissors.

3. Preheat air fryer to 330°F. Arrange pita strips in single layer in basket.

4. Cook pita strips in batches 6 to 8 minutes or until edges are golden brown. Serve with dip, if desired.

BRUSCHETTA

makes 8 servings (1 cup)

4 plum tomatoes, seeded and diced
½ cup packed fresh basil leaves,
  finely chopped
5 tablespoons olive oil, divided
2 cloves garlic, minced
2 teaspoons finely chopped oil-
  packed sun-dried tomatoes

¼ teaspoon salt
⅛ teaspoon black pepper
16 slices Italian bread
2 tablespoons grated Parmesan
  cheese

1. Combine fresh tomatoes, basil, 3 tablespoons oil, garlic, sun-dried tomatoes, salt and pepper in large bowl; mix well. Let stand at room temperature 1 hour to blend flavors.

2. Brush one side of bread slices with remaining 2 tablespoons oil; sprinkle with cheese.

3. Preheat air fryer to 350°F. Place bread in single layer in basket.

4. Cook bread in batches 3 to 5 minutes or until golden brown. Top each bread slice with 1 tablespoon tomato mixture.

GREEN BEAN FRIES

makes 6 servings

DIPPING SAUCE

- ½ **cup mayonnaise**
- ¼ **cup sour cream**
- ¼ **cup buttermilk**
- ¼ **cup minced peeled cucumber**
- 1½ **teaspoons lemon juice**
- 1 **clove garlic**
- 1 **teaspoon wasabi powder**
- 1 **teaspoon prepared horseradish**
- ½ **teaspoon dried dill weed**
- ½ **teaspoon dried parsley flakes**
- ½ **teaspoon salt**
- ⅛ **teaspoon ground red pepper**

GREEN BEAN FRIES

- 8 **ounces fresh green beans, trimmed**
- ⅓ **cup all-purpose flour**
- ⅓ **cup cornstarch**
- ½ **cup milk**
- 1 **egg**
- ¾ **cup plain dry bread crumbs**
- 1 **teaspoon salt**
- ½ **teaspoon onion powder**
- ¼ **teaspoon garlic powder**

1. For sauce, combine mayonnaise, sour cream, buttermilk, cucumber, lemon juice, garlic, wasabi powder, horseradish, dill weed, parsley flakes, salt and red pepper in blender; blend until smooth. Refrigerate until ready to use.

2. For green beans, bring large saucepan of salted water to a boil. Add beans; cook 4 minutes or until crisp-tender. Drain and run under cold water to stop cooking.

3. Combine flour and cornstarch in large bowl. Whisk milk and egg in another large bowl. Combine bread crumbs, salt, onion powder and garlic powder in large shallow dish. Place green beans in flour mixture; toss to coat. Working in batches, coat beans with egg mixture, letting excess drain back into bowl. Roll green beans in bread crumb mixture to coat.

4. Preheat air fryer to 390°F. Cook green beans in batches 6 to 8 minutes or until golden brown, shaking occasionally during cooking. Serve warm with dipping sauce.

TIP: For a quicker dip, substitute prepared ranch dressing for the homemade version.

MEDITERRANEAN BAKED FETA

makes 4 to 6 servings

Savory Pita Chips (recipe follows)
or store-bought pita chips
1 package (8 ounces) feta cheese,
cut crosswise into 4 slices
½ cup grape tomatoes, halved
¼ cup sliced roasted red peppers

¼ cup pitted Kalamata olives
⅛ teaspoon dried oregano
Black pepper
2 tablespoons extra virgin olive oil
1 tablespoon shredded fresh basil

1 Prepare Savory Pita Chips.

2 Preheat air fryer to 370°F.

3 Place cheese in small baking dish that fits inside air fryer; top with tomatoes, roasted peppers and olives. Sprinkle with oregano and black pepper; drizzle with oil.

4 Cook 6 to 8 minutes or until cheese is soft. Sprinkle with basil. Serve immediately with pita chips.

SAVORY PITA CHIPS: Split 2 pita bread rounds in half horizontally; cut each round into six wedges for total of 24 pieces. Spray wedges with nonstick cooking spray; sprinkle with ½ teaspoon basil, ¼ teaspoon garlic powder and ⅛ teaspoon salt. Cook in preheated 350°F air fryer 8 to 10 minutes or until golden brown, shaking occasionally during cooking. Cool completely before serving.

BAGEL CHIPS WITH EVERYTHING SEASONING DIP

makes 2 cups dip (about 16 servings)

2 large bagels, cut vertically into
thin (¼-inch) slices
1 container (12 ounces) whipped
cream cheese
1½ tablespoons green onion, finely
chopped (green part only)

1 teaspoon dried minced onion
1 teaspoon granulated garlic
1 teaspoon sesame seeds
1 teaspoon poppy seeds
¼ teaspoon coarse salt

1 Preheat air fryer to 350°F.

2 Spray bagel slices generously with butter-flavored nonstick cooking spray.

3 Cook bagel slices in batches 7 to 8 minutes or until golden brown, shaking occasionally during cooking.

4 Meanwhile, combine cream cheese, green onion, dried onion, garlic, sesame seeds, poppy seeds and salt in medium bowl; mix well. Serve with bagel chips.

TOASTED TORTELLINI

makes 6 to 8 servings

2 eggs
2 tablespoons milk
⅔ cup Italian seasoned bread crumbs
1 teaspoon garlic powder
2 tablespoons grated Parmesan cheese

½ teaspoon salt
1 package (9 ounces) refrigerated tortellini
Fresh parsley, chopped
Marinara sauce, warmed

1. Whisk eggs and milk in medium bowl until well blended. Combine bread crumbs, garlic powder, cheese and salt in shallow dish; mix well.

2. Dip tortellini in egg mixture, letting excess drip back into bowl. Roll tortellini in bread crumb mixture to coat. Spray with nonstick cooking spray.

3. Preheat air fryer to 370°F. Spray basket with cooking spray.

4. Cook tortellini in single layer 6 to 8 minutes or until golden brown and crisp. (Cook in batches if necessary.) Sprinkle with parsley; serve with marinara sauce.

BUFFALO CAULIFLOWER BITES

makes 4 servings

½ cup all-purpose flour
½ cup water
½ teaspoon garlic powder
½ teaspoon salt
¼ teaspoon black pepper
1 small head cauliflower,
    cut into small florets

3 tablespoons hot pepper sauce
1 tablespoon melted butter
    Chopped fresh parsley (optional)
    Blue cheese dressing and celery
     sticks

1. Combine flour, water, garlic powder, salt and black pepper in large bowl; mix well. Add cauliflower; stir until well coated.

2. Preheat air fryer to 390°F. Line basket with parchment paper.

3. Cook cauliflower 12 to 15 minutes or until slightly tender and browned, shaking occasionally during cooking.

4. Meanwhile, combine hot pepper sauce and butter in large bowl; mix well. Add warm cauliflower; toss to coat. Sprinkle with parsley, if desired. Serve with blue cheese dressing and celery sticks.

CORN TORTILLA CHIPS

makes 3 dozen chips (about 12 servings)

6 (6-inch) corn tortillas, preferably day-old

½ teaspoon salt

Salsa or guacamole (optional)

1. If tortillas are fresh, let stand, uncovered, in single layer on wire rack 1 to 2 hours to dry slightly.

2. Stack tortillas; cut into six wedges. Spray tortillas generously with nonstick cooking spray.

3. Preheat air fryer to 370°F.

4. Cook tortilla wedges in batches 5 to 6 minutes, shaking halfway through cooking. Sprinkle with salt. Serve chips with salsa or guacamole, if desired.

TIP: Serve tortilla chips with salsa or guacamole as a snack, or use as the base for nachos. The chips are best eaten fresh but can be stored, tightly covered, in a cool place for 2 to 3 days.

POULTRY

ZESTY ITALIAN CHICKEN NUGGETS

makes 2 servings

2 **boneless skinless chicken breasts (about 4 ounces each)**
¼ **cup zesty Italian salad dressing**
1 **tablespoon honey**

2 **cloves garlic, minced**
1½ **teaspoons lime juice**
½ **teaspoon salt**
¼ **teaspoon black pepper**

1. Cut chicken into 1-inch pieces. Place in large resealable food storage bag.

2. Whisk dressing, honey, garlic, lime juice, salt and pepper in medium bowl until well blended. Pour over chicken; seal bag and turn to coat. Marinate in refrigerator 30 minutes to 1 hour.

3. Preheat air fryer to 370°F. Line basket with parchment paper. Remove chicken from marinade; discard marinade.

4. Cook chicken 10 to 12 minutes or until cooked through, shaking halfway through cooking.

CHICKEN BACON QUESADILLAS

makes 4 servings

1 cup (4 ounces) shredded
Colby-Jack cheese

4 (8-inch) flour tortillas

1 cup coarsely chopped cooked
chicken

4 slices bacon, crisp-cooked
and coarsely chopped*

½ cup pico de gallo, plus additional
for serving

2 teaspoons vegetable oil
Sour cream and guacamole
(optional)

*Cook bacon in preheated 390°F. air fryer
6 to 8 minutes or until crisp. Remove to
paper towel-lined plate; cool completely
before crumbling.*

1. Sprinkle 2 tablespoons cheese over half of each tortilla. Top with ¼ cup chicken, one fourth of bacon, 2 tablespoons pico de gallo and 2 tablespoons cheese. Fold tortillas in half; brush both sides of quesadillas lightly with oil.

2. Preheat air fryer to 370°F.

3. Cook quesadillas in batches 3 to 4 minutes or until cheese is melted and tortillas are lightly browned. Remove to cutting board; cool slightly.

4. Cut quesadillas into wedges; serve with additional pico de gallo, sour cream and guacamole, if desired.

LEMON-PEPPER CHICKEN

makes 4 servings

⅓ cup lemon juice
¼ cup finely chopped onion
2 tablespoons olive oil
1 tablespoon packed brown sugar
1 tablespoon black pepper

3 cloves garlic, minced
2 teaspoons grated lemon peel
½ teaspoon salt
4 boneless skinless chicken breasts
   (about 4 ounces each)

1. Combine lemon juice, onion, oil, brown sugar, pepper, garlic, lemon peel and salt in small bowl; mix well.

2. Place chicken in large resealable food storage bag; pour marinade over chicken. Seal bag; turn to coat. Refrigerate at least 4 hours or overnight.

3. Preheat air fryer to 370°F. Line basket with parchment paper or foil; spray with nonstick cooking spray. Remove chicken from marinade; discard marinade.

4. Cook chicken in single layer 15 to 20 minutes or until browned and no longer pink in center, turning halfway through cooking. (Cook in batches if necessary.)

BANG BANG CHICKEN

makes 4 servings

CREAMY HOT SAUCE

- ½ **cup mayonnaise**
- ¼ **cup sweet chili sauce**
- 1½ **teaspoons hot pepper sauce**

CHICKEN

- ½ **cup all-purpose flour**
- ¾ **cup panko bread crumbs**
- 1 **pound chicken breasts, cut into 1-inch pieces**
- 2 **green onions, chopped**
  Hot cooked rice (optional)

1. For sauce, combine mayonnaise, chili sauce and hot pepper sauce in medium bowl; mix well. Reserve half of sauce for serving; place remaining half in shallow dish.

2. Place flour in separate shallow dish. Place panko in third shallow dish.

3. Roll chicken in flour to coat. Dip chicken in sauce mixture, then roll in panko to coat. Spray with nonstick cooking spray.

4. Preheat air fryer to 390°F. Line basket with parchment paper.

5. Cook chicken in batches 10 to 12 minutes or until golden brown and cooked through, shaking halfway through cooking. Transfer to large plate; drizzle with reserved sauce. Sprinkle with green onions. Serve with rice, if desired.

GARLICKY AIR-FRIED CHICKEN THIGHS

makes 4 servings

1 egg
2 tablespoons water
1 cup plain dry bread crumbs
1 teaspoon salt
1 teaspoon garlic powder

½ teaspoon black pepper
¼ teaspoon ground red pepper
8 bone-in chicken thighs (about
   3 pounds), skin removed

1. Whisk egg and water in shallow dish. Combine bread crumbs, salt, garlic powder, black pepper and ground red pepper in another shallow dish.

2. Dip chicken in egg mixture; turn to coat. Add to bread crumb mixture; turn to coat, pressing lightly to adhere. Spray chicken with nonstick cooking spray.

3. Preheat air fryer to 390°F.

4. Cook chicken in batches 20 to 22 minutes or until browned and cooked through (165°F), turning halfway through cooking.

VARIATIONS: Substitute seasoned bread crumbs for the plain bread crumbs, garlic powder, ground red pepper, salt and black pepper. Or substitute your favorite dried herbs or spices, such as thyme, sage, oregano, rosemary or Cajun seasoning, for the garlic powder and ground red pepper.

TASTY TURKEY TURNOVERS

makes 6 servings

1 package (about 8 ounces)
   refrigerated crescent roll sheet
2 tablespoons honey mustard,
   plus additional for serving

3 ounces thinly sliced deli turkey
¾ cup broccoli coleslaw mix
1 egg white, beaten

1. Unroll dough on lightly floured surface. Use cookie cutter or drinking glass to cut out 3½-inch circles.

2. Brush dough lightly with 2 tablespoons mustard; top with turkey and coleslaw mix. Brush edges of dough with egg white. Fold circles in half; press edges with tines of fork to seal. Brush tops of turnovers with egg white.

3. Preheat air fryer to 370°F. Spray basket with nonstick cooking spray.

4. Cook turnovers in batches 6 to 7 minutes or until golden brown. Let stand 5 minutes before serving. Serve warm or at room temperature with additional honey mustard, if desired.

PARMESAN-CRUSTED CHICKEN

makes 6 servings

6 boneless skinless chicken breasts (about 4 ounces each)

1¼ cups Italian salad dressing

½ cup grated Parmesan cheese

½ cup finely shredded provolone cheese

¼ cup buttermilk ranch salad dressing

¼ cup (½ stick) butter, melted

1 teaspoon minced garlic

¾ cup panko bread crumbs

1. Pound chicken to ½- to ¾-inch thickness between two sheets of waxed paper or plastic wrap with rolling pin or meat mallet. Place in large resealable food storage bag. Pour Italian dressing over chicken; seal bag and turn to coat. Marinate in refrigerator at least 30 minutes.

2. Preheat air fryer to 370°F. Remove chicken from marinade; discard marinade.

3. Cook chicken in batches 12 to 15 minutes or until no longer pink in center, turning halfway through cooking.

4. Meanwhile, combine Parmesan, provolone, ranch dressing, butter and garlic in large microwavable bowl; microwave on HIGH 30 seconds. Stir mixture; add panko and stir until blended. Turn chicken again; spread cheese mixture over chicken.

5. *Increase air fryer temperature to 390°F.* Cook chicken 2 to 3 minutes or until cheese is melted and topping is browned.

BUFFALO CHICKEN WRAPS

makes 2 servings

2 boneless skinless chicken breasts
(about 4 ounces each)

4 tablespoons buffalo wing sauce,
divided

1 cup broccoli coleslaw mix

2 teaspoons blue cheese dressing

2 (8-inch) whole wheat tortillas,
warmed

1. Place chicken in large resealable food storage bag. Add 2 tablespoons buffalo sauce; seal bag and turn to coat. Marinate in refrigerator 15 minutes.

2. Preheat air fryer to 370°F. Cook chicken 12 to 15 minutes or until no longer pink in center, turning halfway through cooking.

3. Remove chicken to cutting board; let cool 5 to 10 minutes. Slice chicken; combine with remaining 2 tablespoons buffalo sauce in medium bowl.

4. Combine coleslaw mix and blue cheese dressing in medium bowl; mix well. Spoon chicken and coleslaw down center of tortillas; roll up to secure filling. Cut wraps in half diagonally.

TIP: For a less spicy wrap, substitute your favorite barbecue sauce for the buffalo wing sauce.

SPICED CHICKEN WITH ROASTED VEGETABLES

makes 4 servings

3 tablespoons olive oil, divided
1 teaspoon salt
1 teaspoon dried oregano
1 teaspoon paprika
½ teaspoon black pepper
2 cloves garlic, minced
4 boneless skinless chicken breasts (about 4 ounces each)

2 cups Brussels sprouts, trimmed and halved
2 small yellow onions, cut into wedges
1 cup frozen crinkle-cut carrots
Salt and black pepper

1. Combine 2 tablespoons oil, 1 teaspoon salt, oregano, paprika, ½ teaspoon pepper and garlic in small bowl; mix well. Brush over chicken.

2. Preheat air fryer to 370°F.

3. Cook chicken in single layer 12 to 15 minutes or until browned and no longer pink in center, turning halfway through cooking. (Cook in batches if necessary.) Remove to plate; tent with foil to keep warm.

4. Combine Brussels sprouts, onions, carrots and remaining 1 tablespoon oil in medium bowl; toss to coat. Season with salt and pepper.

5. *Increase temperature of air fryer to 390°F.* Cook vegetables in batches 6 to 8 minutes or until tender and lightly browned.

TURKEY DINNER QUESADILLA

makes 1 serving

1 (10- to 12-inch) flour tortilla
2 slices deli turkey
2 slices (1 ounce each) Swiss
    cheese

2 tablespoons whole berry
    cranberry sauce
¼ cup baby spinach

1. Place tortilla on work surface. Cut one slit from outer edge of tortilla to center.

2. Arrange turkey slices, cheese slices, cranberry sauce and spinach in each of four quadrants of tortilla. (See inset photo.) Beginning with cut edge, fold tortilla in quarters, covering each quadrant until entire quesadilla is folded into one large triangle.

3. Preheat air fryer to 370°F. Spray outside of quesadilla with nonstick cooking spray.

4. Cook quesadilla 3 to 5 minutes or until tortilla is lightly browned and begins to crisp.

AIR-FRIED BUTTERMILK CHICKEN FINGERS

makes 4 servings

1½ cups biscuit baking mix
1 cup buttermilk*
1 egg, beaten
12 chicken tenders (about
    1½ pounds), patted dry
⅓ cup mayonnaise

1 tablespoon honey
1 tablespoon Dijon mustard
1 tablespoon packed dark brown
    sugar

*Or substitute 1 tablespoon vinegar or
lemon juice plus enough milk to equal
1 cup. Stir; let stand 5 minutes.*

1. Place biscuit mix in shallow dish. Whisk buttermilk and egg in another shallow dish until blended.

2. Roll chicken tenders in biscuit mix, one at a time, coating all sides. Dip in buttermilk mixture; roll in biscuit mix again to coat.

3. Preheat air fryer to 390°F.

4. Cook chicken in batches 10 to 12 minutes or until golden brown and no longer pink in center, turning halfway through cooking.

5. Meanwhile, whisk mayonnaise, honey, mustard and brown sugar in small bowl until well blended. Serve sauce with chicken for dipping.

BLUE CHEESE STUFFED CHICKEN BREASTS

makes 4 servings

½ **cup crumbled blue cheese**
2 **tablespoons butter, softened,**
   divided
¾ **teaspoon dried thyme**

Salt and black pepper
4 **bone-in skin-on chicken breasts**
1 **tablespoon lemon juice**

1. Combine blue cheese, 1 tablespoon butter and thyme in small bowl; mix well. Season with salt and pepper.

2. Loosen chicken skin by pushing fingers between skin and meat, taking care not to tear skin. Spread cheese mixture under skin; massage skin to spread mixture evenly over chicken breast.

3. Preheat air fryer to 370°F.

4. Melt remaining 1 tablespoon butter in small bowl; stir in lemon juice until blended. Brush mixture over chicken; sprinkle with salt and pepper.

5. Cook chicken in single layer 15 to 20 minutes or until golden brown and cooked through (165°). (Cook in batches if necessary.)

MEAT

RENEGADE STEAK

makes 2 servings

1½ teaspoons coarse salt
½ teaspoon paprika
½ teaspoon black pepper
¼ teaspoon onion powder
¼ teaspoon garlic powder
⅛ teaspoon turmeric

⅛ teaspoon ground red pepper
⅛ teaspoon ground coriander
2 center-cut sirloin, strip or tri-tip steaks (1 inch thick, about 6 ounces each)
1 tablespoon butter, melted

1 Combine salt, paprika, black pepper, onion powder, garlic powder, turmeric, red pepper and coriander in small bowl; mix well. Season both sides of steaks with spice mixture (you will not need all of it); let steaks stand at room temperature 45 minutes before cooking.

2 Preheat air fryer to 390°F.

3 Cook steaks 10 to 12 minutes or until desired doneness,* turning halfway through cooking.

4 Brush steaks with butter; cook 30 seconds to 1 minute. Remove steaks to plate; let rest 5 minutes before serving.

*Temperature for medium rare is about 135°F, medium 145°F, medium well 150°F.

PORK WITH SPICY ORANGE CRANBERRY SAUCE

makes 4 servings

1 teaspoon chili powder
½ teaspoon salt
½ teaspoon ground cumin
¼ teaspoon ground allspice
¼ teaspoon black pepper
4 boneless pork chops (1 inch thick, about 4 ounces each)

2 teaspoons vegetable or canola oil
1 cup whole berry cranberry sauce
½ teaspoon grated orange peel
¼ teaspoon ground cinnamon
⅛ teaspoon red pepper flakes

1. Combine chili powder, salt, cumin, allspice and black pepper in small bowl; mix well. Pat pork chops dry with paper towel. Drizzle with oil; sprinkle both sides of pork with spice mixture, coating evenly.

2. Preheat air fryer to 380°F. Spray basket with nonstick cooking spray.

3. Cook pork chops in single layer 5 minutes; turn and cook 4 minutes or until pork is 145°F and barely pink in center. (Cook in batches if necessary.)

4. Meanwhile, combine cranberry sauce, orange peel, cinnamon and red pepper flakes in small bowl; mix well. Serve sauce with pork chops.

AIR-FRIED BEEF TAQUITOS

makes 6 servings

12 ounces ground beef
¼ cup chopped onion
1 tablespoon taco seasoning mix
6 corn tortillas

⅓ cup shredded Cheddar cheese,
  plus additional for topping
Salsa, guacamole and sour cream
  (optional)

1 Cook beef and onion in large skillet over medium-high heat 6 to 8 minutes or until browned, stirring to break up meat. Drain fat. Stir in taco seasoning mix.

2 Spoon about 2 tablespoons beef mixture down center of each tortilla. Top with 1 tablespoon cheese. Roll up tortillas and filling; secure with toothpicks. Spray with nonstick cooking spray.

3 Preheat air fryer to 370°F.

4 Cook taquitos in single layer 3 to 4 minutes or until tortillas are browned and crisp. Remove toothpicks before serving. Top with salsa, guacamole, sour cream and additional cheese, if desired.

SUBSTITUTION: Substitute ground turkey or plant-based crumbles for the ground beef.

PIZZA CALZONES

makes 7 servings

1 package (about 16 ounces) refrigerated jumbo buttermilk biscuits (8 biscuits)

1 cup (4 ounces) shredded mozzarella cheese

⅓ cup sliced mushrooms

2 ounces pepperoni slices (about 35 slices), quartered

½ cup pizza sauce, plus additional for serving

1 egg, beaten

1 Separate biscuits; set aside one biscuit for decoration, if desired. Roll out remaining biscuits into 7-inch rounds on lightly floured surface.

2 Top half of each round with cheese, mushrooms, pepperoni and 1 tablespoon pizza sauce, leaving ½-inch border. Fold dough over filling to form semicircle; seal edges with fork. Brush top of calzones with egg.

3 To make faces, split remaining biscuit horizontally; cut each half into eight ¼-inch strips. For each calzone, roll two strips of dough into spirals for eyes. Divide remaining two strips of dough into seven pieces for noses. Arrange eyes and noses on tops of calzones; brush with egg.

4 Preheat air fryer to 370°F. Line basket with parchment paper or foil.

5 Cook calzones in batches 6 to 8 minutes or until golden brown. Remove to wire rack; cool 5 minutes. Serve with additional pizza sauce.

STEAK, MUSHROOMS AND ONIONS

makes 4 servings

12 ounces boneless steak,
    cut into 1-inch cubes
8 ounces sliced mushrooms
1 small onion, chopped
3 tablespoons melted butter,
    divided
1 teaspoon Worcestershire sauce

½ teaspoon garlic powder
½ teaspoon salt
¼ teaspoon black pepper
    Hot cooked egg noodles or rice
    (optional)
½ teaspoon dried parsley flakes

1 Combine steak, mushrooms and onion in large bowl. Add 1½ tablespoons butter, Worcestershire sauce and garlic powder; toss to coat.

2 Preheat air fryer to 390°F. Line basket with foil.

3 Cook steak mixture 10 to 12 minutes or until steak is cooked to desired doneness, shaking occasionally during cooking.

4 Transfer to large bowl. Add remaining 1½ tablespoons butter, salt and pepper; mix well. Serve over noodles, if desired. Sprinkle with parsley flakes.

JAMAICAN JERK PORK

makes 4 servings

2 green onions, minced
2 tablespoons olive oil
2 to 3 tablespoons jerk seasoning
Juice and peel of 2 limes
1½ tablespoons soy sauce
2 cloves garlic, minced

1½ teaspoons sugar
¼ teaspoon salt
4 thick bone-in pork chops
(1½ to 2 inches thick,
about 8 ounces each)

1. Combine green onions, oil, jerk seasoning, lime juice, lime peel, soy sauce, garlic, sugar and salt in medium bowl; mix well.

2. Place pork chops in large resealable food storage bag. Pour marinade over pork; seal bag and turn to coat. Refrigerate overnight, turning once or twice.

3. Preheat air fryer to 400°F. Spray basket with nonstick cooking spray. Remove pork from marinade; discard marinade.

4. Cook pork chops in single layer 14 minutes or until pork is 145°F, turning halfway through cooking. (Cook in batches if necessary.) Let stand 5 minutes before serving.

SERVING SUGGESTION: Serve with rice and beans.

GREEK–STYLE STEAK SANDWICHES

makes 4 servings

2 teaspoons Greek seasoning
or dried oregano
1 beef flank steak
(about 1½ pounds)
4 pita bread rounds, cut in half
crosswise

1 small cucumber, thinly sliced
1 tomato, cut into thin wedges
½ cup sliced red onion
½ cup crumbled feta cheese
¼ cup red wine vinaigrette
1 cup plain yogurt

1 Rub Greek seasoning over both sides of steak. Place on plate; cover and refrigerate 30 to 60 minutes.

2 Preheat air fryer to 400°F.

3 Cook steak about 12 minutes for medium rare, turning halfway through cooking. Remove to cutting board; tent with foil and let stand 10 minutes before slicing.

4 Cut steak into thin strips against the grain. Divide meat among pita halves; top with cucumber, tomato, onion and cheese. Drizzle with vinaigrette; serve with yogurt.

ROASTED SAUSAGE WITH WHITE BEANS

makes 4 servings

1 pound uncooked mild or hot
   Italian sausage (4 links)
2 tablespoons extra virgin olive oil
10 fresh sage leaves (about 1 sprig)
2 cloves garlic, minced
1 can (about 14 ounces) diced
   tomatoes

2 cans (about 15 ounces each)
   cannellini beans, rinsed
   and drained
¼ teaspoon salt
⅛ teaspoon black pepper

1 Preheat air fryer to 360°F.

2 Cook sausage in single layer 12 minutes or until browned and cooked through, turning halfway through cooking.

3 Meanwhile, heat oil in large skillet over medium-low heat. Add sage and garlic; cook 2 to 3 minutes or just until garlic begins to turn golden. Add tomatoes; bring to a simmer.

4 Stir in beans, salt and pepper; cook 15 minutes, stirring occasionally. Serve sausage over beans.

BAKED PORK BUNS

makes 10 servings

2 teaspoons vegetable oil
2 cups coarsely chopped bok choy
1 small onion, thinly sliced
1 container (18 ounces) refrigerated shredded barbecue pork

2 packages (10 ounces each) refrigerated jumbo buttermilk biscuits (5 biscuits per package)

1 Heat oil in large skillet over medium-high heat. Add bok choy and onion; cook 8 to 10 minutes or until vegetables are tender, stirring occasionally. Remove from heat; stir in barbecue pork.

2 Lightly flour work surface. Separate biscuits; split each biscuit in half to create two thin biscuits. Flatten each biscuit half into 5-inch circle.

3 Spoon heaping tablespoonful pork mixture onto one side of each circle. Fold dough over filling to form half circle; press edges to seal.

4 Preheat air fryer to 350°F. Line basket with parchment paper; spray with nonstick cooking spray.

5 Cook buns in batches 8 to 10 minutes or until golden brown.

FLANK STEAK WITH ITALIAN SALSA

makes 6 servings

2 tablespoons olive oil

2 teaspoons balsamic vinegar

1 flank steak (about 1½ pounds)

1 tablespoon minced garlic

¾ teaspoon salt, divided

¾ teaspoon black pepper, divided

1 cup diced plum tomatoes

⅓ cup chopped pitted kalamata olives

2 tablespoons chopped fresh basil

1 Whisk oil and vinegar in medium bowl until well blended. Place steak in shallow dish. Spread garlic over steak; sprinkle with ½ teaspoon salt and ½ teaspoon pepper. Spoon 2 tablespoons oil mixture over steak. Marinate at least 20 minutes at room temperature or up to 2 hours in refrigerator.

2 Add tomatoes, olives, basil, remaining ¼ teaspoon salt and ¼ teaspoon pepper to remaining 2 teaspoons vinegar mixture in bowl; mix well.

3 Preheat air fryer to 400°F. Remove steak from marinade; discard marinade. (Leave garlic on steak.)

4 Cook steak about 12 minutes for medium rare, turning halfway through cooking. Remove to cutting board; tent with foil and let stand 10 minutes before slicing.

5 Cut steak diagonally into thin slices against the grain. Serve with tomato mixture.

MILANESE PORK CHOPS

makes 4 servings

2 tablespoons all-purpose flour
½ teaspoon salt
½ teaspoon black pepper
1 egg
1 teaspoon water

¼ cup seasoned dry bread crumbs
¼ cup grated Parmesan cheese
4 boneless pork loin chops
  (¾ inch thick)
Lemon wedges

1 Combine flour, salt and pepper in shallow bowl; mix well. Whisk egg and water in another shallow bowl. Combine bread crumbs and cheese in third shallow bowl.

2 Dip each pork chop to coat both sides, first in flour mixture, then in egg mixture, letting excess drip back into bowl. Roll in bread crumb mixture to coat, pressing coating into pork. Place on waxed paper-lined plate; refrigerate 15 minutes.

3 Preheat air fryer to 400°F. Place pork chops in single layer in basket; spray lightly with nonstick cooking spray.

4 Cook pork chops 7 minutes; turn and cook 5 minutes or until pork is 145°F. Serve with lemon wedges.

SEAFOOD

BOURBON–MARINATED SALMON

makes 4 servings

¼ cup packed brown sugar
¼ cup bourbon
¼ cup soy sauce
2 tablespoons lime juice
1 tablespoon grated fresh ginger

1 tablespoon minced garlic
¼ teaspoon black pepper
4 salmon fillets (4 ounces each)
2 tablespoons minced green onion

1. Whisk brown sugar, bourbon, soy sauce, lime juice, ginger, garlic and pepper in medium bowl until well blended. Reserve ¼ cup mixture for serving; set aside.

2. Place fish in large resealable food storage bag. Pour remaining marinade over fish; seal bag and turn to coat. Marinate in refrigerator 2 to 4 hours, turning occasionally.

3. Preheat air fryer to 390°F. Remove fish from marinade; discard marinade.

4. Cook fish in single layer 8 to 10 minutes or until fish begins to flake when tested with fork. (Cook in batches if necessary.) Brush with reserved marinade mixture; sprinkle with green onion.

PARMESAN-CRUSTED TILAPIA

makes 6 servings

⅔ cup plus 2 tablespoons grated
    Parmesan cheese, divided
⅔ cup panko bread crumbs
⅓ cup prepared Alfredo sauce
    (refrigerated or jarred)

1½ teaspoons dried parsley flakes
6 tilapia fillets (4 to 6 ounces each)
    Shaved Parmesan cheese
    (optional)
    Minced fresh parsley (optional)

1. Combine ⅔ cup grated cheese and panko in medium bowl; mix well. Combine Alfredo sauce, remaining 2 tablespoons grated cheese and parsley flakes in small bowl; mix well.

2. Spread Alfredo sauce mixture over top of fish, coating in thick even layer. Top with panko mixture, pressing in gently to adhere.

3. Preheat air fryer to 390°F. Line basket with foil or parchment paper; spray with nonstick cooking spray.

4. Cook fish in batches 8 to 10 minutes or until crust is golden brown and fish begins to flake when tested with fork. Garnish with shaved cheese and fresh parsley.

COCONUT SHRIMP

makes 4 servings

DIPPING SAUCE

- ½ **cup orange marmalade**
- ⅓ **cup Thai chili sauce**
- 1 **teaspoon prepared horseradish**
- ½ **teaspoon salt**

SHRIMP

- 1 **cup flat beer**
- 1 **cup all-purpose flour**
- 2 **cups sweetened flaked coconut, divided**
- 2 **tablespoons sugar**
- 16 **to 20 large raw shrimp, peeled and deveined (with tails on), patted dry**

1. For sauce, whisk marmalade, chili sauce, horseradish and salt in small bowl until well blended.

2. For shrimp, whisk beer, flour, ½ cup coconut and sugar in large bowl until well blended. Place remaining 1½ cups coconut in medium bowl.

3. Dip shrimp in beer batter, then in coconut, turning to coat completely.

4. Preheat air fryer to 390°F. Line basket with parchment paper; spray with nonstick cooking spray.

5. Cook shrimp in batches 6 to 8 minutes or until golden brown, turning halfway through cooking. Serve with dipping sauce.

BAKED CATFISH WITH PEACH AND CUCUMBER SALSA

makes 4 servings

4 catfish fillets (4 ounces each), patted dry
½ teaspoon Italian seasoning
2½ tablespoons fresh bread crumbs

2 teaspoons butter, melted
½ cup peach or mango salsa
3 tablespoons coarsely chopped peeled cucumber

1. Preheat air fryer to 390°F. Line basket with parchment paper; spray with nonstick cooking spray.

2. Place fish in single layer in basket; sprinkle with Italian seasoning and bread crumbs. Drizzle with butter.

3. Cook fish 10 to 12 minutes or until fish begins to flake when tested with fork.

4. Meanwhile, combine salsa and cucumber in small bowl; mix well. Serve with fish.

TERIYAKI SALMON

makes 2 servings

¼ cup dark sesame oil
Juice of 1 lemon
¼ cup soy sauce
2 tablespoons packed brown sugar
1 clove garlic, minced

2 salmon fillets (about 4 ounces each)
Hot cooked rice
Toasted sesame seeds and finely chopped green onion (optional)

1. Whisk oil, lemon juice, soy sauce, brown sugar and garlic in medium bowl until well blended.

2. Place fish in large resealable food storage bag. Pour marinade over fish; seal bag and turn to coat. Refrigerate at least 2 hours.

3. Preheat air fryer to 390°F. Spray basket with nonstick cooking spray.

4. Cook fish 8 to 10 minutes or until top is lightly browned and fish begins to flake when tested with fork. Serve with rice; garnish with sesame seeds and green onion.

BIG KID SHRIMP

makes 4 servings

½ cup plain dry bread crumbs
¼ cup grated Parmesan cheese
½ teaspoon paprika
½ teaspoon salt
⅛ teaspoon black pepper
2 tablespoons butter, melted

1 pound large raw shrimp, peeled and deveined (with tails on)
½ cup mayonnaise
½ cup ketchup
1 tablespoon sweet pickle relish

1. Combine bread crumbs, cheese, paprika, salt and pepper in large bowl; mix well. Stir in butter until blended. Add shrimp; turn to coat, pressing crumb mixture into shrimp to adhere.

2. Preheat air fryer to 390°F. Line basket with parchment paper; spray with nonstick cooking spray.

3. Cook shrimp in batches 5 to 7 minutes or until coating is lightly browned and shrimp are pink and opaque, turning halfway through cooking.

4. Meanwhile, combine mayonnaise, ketchup and relish in small bowl; mix well. Serve with shrimp.

AIR–FRIED CAJUN BASS

makes 4 servings

2 tablespoons all-purpose flour
1 to 1½ teaspoons Cajun seasoning
1 egg white
2 teaspoons water
⅓ cup seasoned dry bread crumbs
2 tablespoons cornmeal

4 skinless striped bass, halibut or
   cod fillets (4 to 6 ounces each),
   thawed if frozen
Chopped fresh parsley (optional)
4 lemon wedges

1 Combine flour and Cajun seasoning in resealable food storage bag. Whisk egg white and water in small bowl. Combine bread crumbs and cornmeal in another small bowl.

2 Working with one at a time, add fillet to bag; shake to coat. Dip in egg white mixture, letting excess drip back into bowl. Roll in bread crumb mixture to coat, pressing lightly to adhere. Place on plate.

3 Preheat air fryer to 390°F.

4 Cook fish in single layer 8 to 10 minutes or until golden brown and opaque in center, turning halfway through cooking. (Cook in batches if necessary.) Sprinkle with parsley, if desired. Serve with lemon wedges.

ROASTED DILL SCROD WITH ASPARAGUS

makes 4 servings

1 teaspoon olive oil
1 bunch (12 ounces) asparagus
   spears, ends trimmed
¾ teaspoon salt, divided
1 tablespoon lemon juice

4 scrod or cod fillets
   (about 5 ounces each)
1 teaspoon dried dill weed
¼ teaspoon black pepper
   Paprika (optional)

1. Preheat air fryer to 390°F. Line basket with parchment paper.

2. Drizzle oil over asparagus; roll spears to coat lightly with oil. Sprinkle with ¼ teaspoon salt. Cook 8 to 10 minutes or until asparagus is tender, shaking halfway through cooking. Remove to plate; keep warm.

3. Drizzle lemon juice over fish. Combine dill weed, remaining ½ teaspoon salt and pepper in small bowl; sprinkle over fish.

4. Cook fish in single layer 10 to 12 minutes or until fish is opaque in center and begins to flake when tested with fork. (Cook in batches if necessary.) Sprinkle with paprika, if desired. Serve with asparagus.

BACON–WRAPPED TERIYAKI SHRIMP

makes 6 servings

1 pound large raw shrimp, peeled
  and deveined (with tails on)
¼ cup teriyaki marinade

12 slices bacon, cut in half crosswise
  (do not use thick-cut bacon)

1. Place shrimp in large resealable food storage bag. Add teriyaki marinade; seal bag and turn to coat. Marinate in refrigerator 15 to 20 minutes.

2. Remove shrimp from bag; reserve marinade. Wrap each shrimp with one piece bacon. Brush bacon with some of reserved marinade.

3. Preheat air fryer to 390°F. Line basket with parchment paper or foil; spray with nonstick cooking spray.

4. Cook shrimp in batches 4 to 6 minutes or until bacon is crisp and shrimp are pink and opaque, turning halfway through cooking.

TIP: Make sure to use regular bacon for this recipe; thick-cut bacon will not be completely cooked when the shrimp are cooked through.

AIR-FRIED SALMON NUGGETS WITH BROCCOLI

makes 5 servings

2 eggs
1 cup plain dry bread crumbs
¾ teaspoon salt, divided
1 pound skinless salmon fillet,
    cut into 1-inch pieces

2 cups broccoli florets
1 tablespoon olive oil
    Sweet and sour sauce or favorite
    dipping sauce (optional)

1. Whisk eggs in small bowl. Combine bread crumbs and ½ teaspoon salt in shallow dish. Dip fish in eggs, letting excess drip back into bowl. Roll in bread crumbs to coat all sides, pressing gently to adhere. Set fish on plate; spray lightly with nonstick cooking spray.

2. Preheat air fryer to 390°F. Spray basket with cooking spray.

3. Cook fish in batches 4 minutes. Turn fish; spray with cooking spray. Cook 3 to 4 minutes or until golden brown. Remove to plate; keep warm.

4. Meanwhile, place broccoli in large bowl; drizzle with oil and toss to coat. Sprinkle with remaining ¼ teaspoon salt.

5. Cook broccoli 6 to 8 minutes or until browned and crisp, shaking halfway through cooking. Serve salmon and broccoli with sweet and sour sauce, if desired.

SUBSTITUTION: Substitute garlic-herb or Italian-seasoned bread crumbs for plain.

BLACKENED CATFISH WITH EASY TARTAR SAUCE

makes 4 servings

Easy Tartar Sauce (recipe follows)
4 catfish fillets (4 ounces each)
2 teaspoons lemon juice

2 teaspoons blackened or Cajun seasoning
Hot cooked rice (optional)

1. Prepare Easy Tartar Sauce.

2. Preheat air fryer to 390°F.

3. Rinse fish and pat dry with paper towel. Sprinkle with lemon juice; spray with nonstick cooking spray. Sprinkle with seasoning blend; spray again with cooking spray.

4. Cook fish in single layer 8 to 10 minutes or until fish begins to flake when tested with fork, turning halfway through cooking. (Cook in batches if necessary.) Serve with tartar sauce and rice, if desired.

EASY TARTAR SAUCE: Combine ¼ cup mayonnaise, 2 teaspoons sweet pickle relish and 1 teaspoon lemon juice in small bowl; mix well. Cover and refrigerate until ready to serve.

MEATLESS MEALS

VEGETABLE AND CHEESE SANDWICHES

makes 2 servings

1 large zucchini, cut lengthwise into eight ¼-inch slices

2 slices sweet onion (such as Vidalia or Walla Walla), cut into ¼-inch slices

1 yellow bell pepper, cut lengthwise into quarters

4 tablespoons Caesar salad dressing, divided

4 slices sourdough bread

2 slices (1 ounce each) Muenster cheese

1. Preheat air fryer to 370°F. Spray basket with nonstick cooking spray.

2. Combine zucchini, onion, bell pepper and 2 tablespoons dressing in medium bowl; toss to coat.

3. Cook vegetables 6 to 8 minutes or until tender and lightly browned. Remove to plate.

4. Brush both sides of bread lightly with remaining 2 tablespoons dressing. Cook bread in single layer 2 minutes or until lightly browned. Top two slices bread with two slices cheese.

5. Arrange vegetables over cheese-topped bread slices; top with remaining bread. Cook sandwiches 1 minute or until cheese is slightly melted.

EGGPLANT PIZZAS

makes 4 servings

1 egg
1 tablespoon water
¾ cup Italian-seasoned dry bread
   crumbs
1 medium eggplant, cut crosswise
   into ½-inch slices

½ cup marinara sauce
½ cup (2 ounces) shredded
   mozzarella cheese
Chopped fresh basil

1. Whisk egg and water in shallow dish. Place bread crumbs in another shallow dish. Dip eggplant in egg mixture, letting excess drip back into dish. Coat with bread crumbs, pressing gently to adhere. Spray with nonstick cooking spray.

2. Preheat air fryer to 370°F. Line basket with foil.

3. Cook eggplant in batches 10 to 12 minutes or until slightly tender and golden brown.

4. Top each eggplant slice with 1 tablespoon marinara sauce and 1 tablespoon cheese. Cook 3 to 5 minutes or until cheese is melted and beginning to brown. Sprinkle with basil just before serving.

TIP: Add chopped bell peppers, sliced tomatoes, olives or any other favorite topping to the pizzas with the marinana sauce.

BARBECUE CAULIFLOWER CALZONES

makes 4 servings

1 head cauliflower, cut into florets
   and thinly sliced
2 tablespoons olive oil
   Salt and black pepper
¾ cup barbecue sauce, plus
   additional for serving
1 container (about 14 ounces)
   refrigerated pizza dough

½ onion, chopped
1 cup (4 ounces) shredded
   mozzarella cheese
   Ranch or blue cheese dressing
   (optional)

1 Preheat air fryer to 390°F.

2 Place cauliflower in large bowl. Drizzle with oil and season lightly with salt and pepper; toss to coat.

3 Cook cauliflower 6 to 8 minutes or until slightly tender and lightly browned, shaking halfway through cooking. Return to bowl; stir in ¾ cup barbecue sauce. *Reduce temperature of air fryer to 370°F.*

4 Unroll dough on lightly floured cutting board. Stretch dough into 11×17-inch rectangle; cut into quarters. Place one fourth of onion on half of each piece of dough. Top with one fourth of cauliflower and ¼ cup cheese. Fold dough over filling; roll and pinch edges to seal. Spray with nonstick cooking spray.

5 Cook calzones in batches 5 to 7 minutes or until golden brown. Serve with additional barbecue sauce and ranch dressing, if desired.

STUFFED AIR-FRIED AVOCADO

makes 2 servings

⅓ cup seasoned panko bread
    crumbs
1 large avocado, pitted and peeled
    Salt and black pepper
5 cherry tomatoes, halved
¼ cup shredded mozzarella cheese

2 tablespoons grated Parmesan
    cheese
2 tablespoons chopped fresh
    basil leaves
    Balsamic glaze

1. Preheat air fryer to 370°F. Line basket with foil.

2. Place panko in shallow dish. Press avocado halves into panko, turning to coat completely. Season with salt and pepper; spray with nonstick cooking spray.

3. Cook avocado 6 to 8 minutes or until panko is lightly browned.

4. Meanwhile, combine tomatoes, mozzarella, Parmesan and basil in medium bowl, mix well. Divide mixture between avocado halves.

5. Cook 1 to 2 minutes or until cheese is melted. Drizzle with balsamic glaze; serve immediately.

ROASTED VEGETABLE AND HUMMUS SANDWICH

makes 8 servings

1 small eggplant, cut lengthwise into ⅛-inch slices

1 yellow squash, cut lengthwise into ⅛-inch slices

1 zucchini, cut diagonally into ⅛-inch slices

1 tablespoon extra virgin olive oil

½ teaspoon salt

¼ teaspoon black pepper

1 boule or round bread (8 inches), cut in half horizontally

1 container (8 ounces) hummus, any flavor

1 jar (12 ounces) roasted red peppers, drained

1 jar (6 ounces) marinated artichoke hearts, drained and chopped

1 small tomato, thinly sliced

1. Preheat air fryer to 390°F. Combine eggplant, squash, zucchini, oil, salt and black pepper in large bowl; toss to coat.

2. Cook vegetables in batches 4 to 6 minutes or until tender and golden brown, shaking halfway through cooking. Cool to room temperature.

3. Scoop out bread from both halves of loaf, leaving about 1 inch of bread on edges and about 1½ inches on bottom. (Reserve bread for bread crumbs or croutons.)

4. Spread hummus evenly over bottom of bread. Layer vegetables, roasted peppers, artichokes and tomato over hummus; cover with top half of bread. Wrap stuffed loaf tightly in plastic wrap; refrigerate at least 1 hour before cutting into wedges.

TIP: To prepare your own roasted red peppers in the air fryer instead of using jarred peppers, preheat the air fryer to 390°F. Place one large red bell pepper in the basket; cook 15 minutes, turning once or twice. Let the pepper stand in the air fryer 10 minutes to loosen the skin. Remove the skin with a paring knife under running water. Cut the pepper in half; remove and discard the stem and seeds. Cut into strips.

CAPRESE PORTOBELLOS

makes 4 servings

2 tablespoons butter
½ teaspoon minced garlic
1 teaspoon dried parsley flakes
4 portobello mushrooms,
   stems removed
1 cup (4 ounces) shredded
   mozzarella cheese

1 cup cherry or grape tomatoes,
   thinly sliced
2 tablespoons fresh basil,
   thinly sliced
   Balsamic glaze or balsamic
   vinegar

1. Combine butter, garlic and parsley flakes in small microwavable dish. Microwave on LOW (30%) 30 seconds or until butter is melted. Stir until well blended.

2. Preheat air fryer to 390°F. Spray basket with nonstick cooking spray.

3. Brush both sides of mushrooms with butter mixture.

4. Fill each mushroom cap with ¼ cup cheese; top with tomatoes.

5. Cook 5 to 7 minutes or until cheese is melted and lightly browned. Top with basil; drizzle with balsamic glaze.

BLACK BEAN AND RICE STUFFED POBLANO PEPPERS

makes 4 servings

4 poblano peppers
1 can (about 15 ounces) black
    beans, rinsed and drained
1 cup cooked brown rice

¾ cup shredded Cheddar cheese or
    pepper-Jack cheese, divided
⅔ cup chunky salsa
¼ teaspoon salt

1. Cut thin slice from one side of each pepper; remove seeds and membranes. Chop pepper slices; set aside.

2. Preheat air fryer to 380°F. Spray peppers with nonstick cooking spray.

3. Cook peppers in single layer 6 to 8 minutes or until skin is slightly softened. (Cook in batches if necessary.) Remove to plate. *Reduce temperature of air fryer to 350°F.*

4. Combine beans, rice, ½ cup cheese, salsa, chopped poblano pepper and salt in medium bowl; mix well. Spoon mixture into peppers, mounding in center.

5. Line basket with parchment paper; place stuffed peppers in single layer in basket.

6. Cook peppers 6 to 8 minutes or until filling is heated through. Sprinkle with remaining ¼ cup cheese; cook 2 minutes or until cheese is melted.

MUSHROOM PO' BOYS

makes 4 servings

Remoulade Sauce*
  (recipe follows)
1 cup buttermilk
1 tablespoon hot pepper sauce
1¼ cups all-purpose flour
1 teaspoon salt
1 teaspoon smoked paprika
¼ teaspoon onion powder
¼ teaspoon black pepper

1 package (4 ounces) sliced
  shiitake mushrooms
1 package (3 ounces) oyster
  mushrooms, cut into 2-inch
  or bite-size pieces
1 loaf French bread, ends trimmed,
  cut into 4 pieces and split
Sliced fresh tomatoes and finely
  shredded iceberg lettuce

Or substitute mayonnaise.

1. Prepare Remoulade Sauce; cover and refrigerate until ready to use.

2. Combine buttermilk and 1 tablespoon hot pepper sauce in medium bowl. Combine flour, salt, paprika, onion powder and black pepper in another medium bowl; mix well. Dip mushroom pieces, a few at a time, in buttermilk mixture; roll in flour mixture to coat. Dip again in buttermilk mixture and roll in flour mixture; place on plate. Repeat until all mushrooms are coated.

3. Preheat air fryer to 370°F. Line basket with parchment paper; spray with nonstick cooking spray.

4. Place mushrooms in single layer in basket; spray tops with cooking spray.

5. Cook mushrooms in batches 8 to 10 minutes or until coating is crisp and browned, shaking halfway through cooking. Serve mushrooms on bread with tomatoes, lettuce and sauce.

REMOULADE SAUCE: Combine ½ cup mayonnaise, 2 tablespoons Dijon or coarse grain mustard, 1 tablespoon lemon juice, 1 clove garlic, minced and ½ teaspoon hot pepper sauce in small bowl; mix well.

CORNMEAL–CRUSTED CAULIFLOWER STEAKS

makes 4 servings

½ **cup cornmeal**
¼ **cup all-purpose flour**
1 **teaspoon salt**
1 **teaspoon dried sage**
½ **teaspoon garlic powder**

¼ **teaspoon black pepper**
½ **cup milk**
2 **heads cauliflower**
2 **tablespoons butter, melted**
   Barbecue sauce (optional)

1 Combine cornmeal, flour, salt, sage, garlic powder and pepper in shallow dish; mix well. Pour milk into another shallow dish.

2 Turn cauliflower stem side up on cutting board. Trim away leaves, leaving stem intact. Cut through stem into three slices. Trim off excess florets from end slices, creating flat "steaks." Repeat with remaining cauliflower. Reserve extra cauliflower for another use.

3 Dip cauliflower into milk to coat both sides. Place in cornmeal mixture; pat onto all sides of cauliflower, pressing to adhere. Drizzle with butter.

4 Preheat air fryer to 390°F. Line basket with parchment paper.

5 Cook cauliflower in batches 12 to 15 minutes or until tender, turning halfway through cooking. Serve with barbecue sauce, if desired.

SPICY EGGPLANT BURGERS

makes 4 servings

1 eggplant (about 1¼ pounds)

2 egg whites

½ cup Italian-style panko bread crumbs

3 tablespoons chipotle mayonnaise or regular mayonnaise

4 whole wheat hamburger buns, toasted

1 cup loosely packed baby spinach

8 thin slices tomato

4 slices pepper jack cheese

1. Cut four (½-inch-thick) slices crosswise from widest part of eggplant. Beat egg whites in shallow dish. Place panko in another shallow dish.

2. Dip eggplant in egg whites; coat with panko, pressing gently to adhere. Spray with nonstick cooking spray.

3. Preheat air fryer to 370°F. Line basket with foil.

4. Cook eggplant in single layer 8 to 10 minutes or until golden brown, turning halfway through cooking. (Cook in batches if necessary.)

5. Spread mayonnaise on bottom halves of buns; top with spinach, tomato, eggplant, cheese and tops of buns.

BELL PEPPER AND RICOTTA CALZONES

makes 6 servings

1 tablespoon olive oil
1 medium red bell pepper, chopped
1 medium green bell pepper, chopped
1 small onion, chopped
½ teaspoon Italian seasoning
¼ teaspoon salt

⅛ teaspoon black pepper
1 clove garlic, minced
1¼ cups marinara sauce, divided
¼ cup ricotta cheese
⅛ cup mozzarella cheese
1 package (about 14 ounces) refrigerated pizza dough

1. Heat oil in large nonstick skillet over medium heat. Add bell peppers, onion, Italian seasoning, salt and black pepper; cook about 8 minutes or until vegetables are tender, stirring occasionally. Add garlic; cook and stir 1 minute. Stir in ½ cup marinara sauce; cook about 2 minutes or until thickened slightly. Transfer to medium bowl; let cool slightly.

2. Combine ricotta and mozzarella in small bowl; mix well. Unroll pizza dough on cutting board or work surface. Cut into six 4-inch squares; pat each square into 5-inch square.

3. Spoon ⅓ cup vegetable mixture into center of each square; top with 1 tablespoon cheese mixture. Fold dough over filling to form triangle; pinch and fold edges together to seal.

4. Preheat air fryer to 370°F. Line basket with parchment paper.

5. Cook calzones in batches 8 to 10 minutes or until lightly browned. Cool on wire rack 5 minutes; serve with remaining marinara sauce.

VEGETABLES

GREEN BEANS AND MUSHROOMS

makes 4 to 6 servings

1 **pound fresh green beans, trimmed**
1 **large onion, cut into ¼-inch slices**
8 **ounces sliced mushrooms**
1 **teaspoon minced garlic**

½ **teaspoon salt**
¼ **teaspoon black pepper**
1 **tablespoon olive oil**

1 Preheat air fryer to 370°F. Spray basket with nonstick cooking spray.

2 Combine green beans, onion, mushrooms, garlic, salt and pepper in large bowl. Drizzle with oil; toss to coat.

3 Cook vegetables 14 to 16 minutes or until tender and browned, shaking halfway through cooking.

AIR-FRYER MEXICAN CORN RIBS

makes 4 servings

2 ears corn
¼ cup (½ stick) butter, softened
½ teaspoon chili powder
¼ teaspoon garlic powder
¼ teaspoon black pepper
¼ cup mayonnaise

2 teaspoons lime juice
1 teaspoon hot pepper sauce
2 tablespoons crumbled cotija
 or feta cheese
1 tablespoon chopped fresh cilantro

1. Husk corn and remove silk. Rinse and dry corn. Use large knife to cut ears of corn in half horizontally, then cut each half lengthwise into quarters to create four "ribs."

2. Combine butter, chili powder, garlic powder and black pepper in small bowl; mix well. Brush mixture over corn.

3. Preheat air fryer to 390°F. Line basket with parchment paper.

4. Cook corn 12 to 14 minutes or until charred, turning halfway through cooking. Transfer to plate.

5. Meanwhile, whisk mayonnaise, lime juice and hot pepper sauce in small bowl until well blended. Brush over hot corn; sprinkle with cheese and cilantro.

EGGPLANT STEAKS

makes 4 to 6 servings

1 small to medium eggplant,
  cut crosswise into
  ¾-inch slices
2 tablespoons olive oil
1 tablespoon herb seasoning blend
  or garlic herb seasoning
¼ cup (½ stick) butter, melted
1 tablespoon minced garlic

½ teaspoon salt
¼ teaspoon black pepper
1 tablespoon grated Parmesan
  cheese, plus additional for
  garnish
1 tablespoon fresh chopped parsley
  Marinara sauce, warmed (optional)

1 Preheat air fryer to 390°F. Spray basket with nonstick cooking spray.

2 Place eggplant on large plate. Brush both sides with oil; sprinkle with seasoning blend.

3 Cook eggplant in single layer 14 to 16 minutes or until golden brown and crisp around edges, turning halfway through cooking. (Cook in batches if necessary.)

4 Combine butter, garlic, salt, pepper and cheese in small bowl; mix well. Brush over warm eggplant; sprinkle with parsley and additional cheese. Serve with marinara sauce, if desired.

GARLIC AIR-FRIED FRIES

makes 4 servings

2 large potatoes, peeled and cut
    into matchstick strips
2 teaspoons plus 1 tablespoon
    olive oil, divided
1½ teaspoons minced garlic
½ teaspoon dried parsley flakes

½ teaspoon salt
¼ teaspoon ground black pepper
    Ketchup, blue cheese dressing
    and/or ranch dressing
    (optional)

1. Combine potatoes and 2 teaspoons oil in medium bowl; toss to coat.

2. Preheat air fryer to 390°F. Line basket with parchment paper.

3. Cook potatoes in batches 8 to 10 minutes or until golden brown and crisp, shaking occasionally during cooking.

4. Meanwhile, combine remaining 1 tablespoon oil, garlic, parsley flakes, salt and pepper in large bowl; mix well.

5. Add warm fries to garlic mixture; toss to coat. Serve immediately with ketchup and/or dressing, if desired.

AIR-FRIED CAULIFLOWER FLORETS >>

makes 4 servings

1 head cauliflower, cut into florets
1 tablespoon olive oil
3 tablespoons grated Parmesan
cheese

2 tablespoons panko bread crumbs
½ teaspoon salt
½ teaspoon chopped fresh parsley
¼ teaspoon ground black pepper

1. Place cauliflower in large bowl; drizzle with oil. Sprinkle with cheese, panko, salt, parsley and pepper; toss to coat.

2. Preheat air fryer to 390°F. Spray basket with nonstick cooking spray.

3. Cook cauliflower in batches 12 to 15 minutes or until lightly browned, shaking every 5 minutes.

CINNAMON HONEY GLAZED CARROTS

makes 6 servings

¼ cup honey
2 tablespoons butter
1 teaspoon ground cinnamon
½ teaspoon ground nutmeg

Pinch salt
1 package (16 ounces) carrot chips
or baby carrots

1. Combine honey and butter in medium microwavable bowl; microwave on HIGH 30 seconds or until melted. Add cinnamon, nutmeg and salt; mix well.

2. Add carrots to honey mixture; toss to coat.

3. Preheat air fryer to 390°F. Line basket with parchment paper.

4. Cook carrots in single layer 12 to 15 minutes or until browned and slightly tender, shaking halfway through cooking. (Cook in batches if necessary.)

HERB ROASTED POTATOES AND ONIONS

makes 6 servings

2 pounds unpeeled red potatoes, cut into 1½-inch pieces

1 sweet onion, such as Vidalia or Walla Walla, coarsely chopped

2 tablespoons olive oil

2 cloves garlic, minced

½ teaspoon salt

¼ teaspoon black pepper

¼ cup packed chopped mixed fresh herbs, such as basil, chives, parsley, oregano, rosemary leaves, sage, tarragon and thyme

1. Place potatoes and onion in large bowl. Combine oil, garlic, salt and pepper in small bowl; mix well. Drizzle over vegetables; toss to coat.

2. Preheat air fryer to 390°F. Line basket with foil.

3. Cook vegetables in batches 18 to 20 minutes or until potatoes are tender and browned, shaking occasionally during cooking.

4. Transfer vegetables to large bowl. Add fresh herbs; toss to coat.

GARLIC AIR-FRIED MUSHROOMS

makes 4 servings

1 pound mushrooms, trimmed
  and halved
2 tablespoons olive oil
1 teaspoon garlic powder
1 teaspoon Italian seasoning

½ teaspoon salt
¼ teaspoon black pepper
  Fresh chopped parsley
  Lemon wedges (optional)

1. Preheat air fryer to 370°F.

2. Combine mushrooms, oil, garlic powder, Italian seasoning, salt and pepper in large bowl; toss to coat.

3. Cook mushrooms 12 to 15 minutes or until tender and browned, shaking occasionally during cooking. Sprinkle with parsley; serve with lemon wedges, if desired.

BUTTERNUT SQUASH FRIES

makes 4 servings

½ **teaspoon garlic powder**
¼ **teaspoon salt**
¼ **teaspoon ground red pepper**

1 **butternut squash (about 2½ pounds), peeled, seeded and cut into thin slices about 2 inches long**
2 **teaspoons vegetable oil**

1. Preheat air fryer to 390°F.

2. Combine garlic powder, salt and red pepper in small bowl; mix well.

3. Place squash in large bowl. Drizzle with oil and sprinkle with seasoning mix; toss gently to coat.

4. Cook squash in batches 16 to 18 minutes or until tender and beginning to brown, shaking halfway through cooking.

PUMPKIN PARMESAN TWICE–BAKED POTATOES

makes 4 servings

2 baking potatoes (about 12 ounces each)

1 cup shredded Parmesan cheese, plus additional for garnish

⅓ cup half-and-half

¼ cup canned pumpkin

1½ teaspoons minced fresh sage *or* ¼ teaspoon dried thyme

¼ teaspoon salt

⅛ teaspoon black pepper

1. Preheat air fryer to 400°F. Scrub potatoes; pierce in several places with fork or small knife.

2. Cook potatoes 25 minutes; turn and cook 15 to 20 minutes or until soft.

3. When cool enough to handle, cut potatoes in half lengthwise. Scoop out most of potato pulp into medium bowl, leaving thin potato shell. Mash potatoes with fork. Add 1 cup cheese, half-and-half, pumpkin, sage, salt and pepper; mix well.

4. Spoon pumpkin mixture into potato shells. Cook potatoes 5 minutes or until filling is heated through. Sprinkle with additional cheese, if desired.

FRIED ZUCCHINI

makes 4 to 6 servings

1 package (about 10 ounces)
  zucchini noodles
¼ cup all-purpose flour
½ teaspoon Italian seasoning

¼ teaspoon salt
1 egg, beaten
¾ cup panko bread crumbs
  Marinara sauce, warmed (optional)

1 Drain excess water from zucchini noodles; place in medium bowl. Cut into shorter pieces with scissors. Add flour, Italian seasoning and salt; toss to coat. Add egg; stir until well blended.

2 Place panko in shallow dish.

3 Shape zucchini mixture into 1-inch balls. Add to dish with panko; turn to coat, pressing gently to adhere.

4 Preheat air fryer to 390°F. Line basket with parchment paper; spray with nonstick cooking spray.

5 Cook zucchini in batches 8 to 10 minutes or until golden brown, turning halfway through cooking. Serve warm with marinara sauce, if desired.

CRISPY BRUSSELS SPROUTS >>

makes 4 servings

1 pound Brussels sprouts,
   trimmed and halved
1½ tablespoons olive oil
2 tablespoons grated Parmesan
   cheese

¼ cup ground almonds
1 tablespoon everything bagel
   seasoning or seasoning
   of your choice

1. Preheat air fryer to 370°F.

2. Combine Brussels sprouts, oil, cheese, almonds and bagel seasoning in medium bowl; toss to coat.

3. Cook Brussels sprouts in batches 8 to 10 minutes or until lightly browned and crisp, shaking occasionally during cooking.

AIR-FRIED CORN ON THE COB

makes 2 servings

1 tablespoon butter, melted
¼ teaspoon salt
¼ teaspoon black pepper

2 ears corn, husks and silks
   removed
Grated Parmesan cheese
   (optional)

1. Preheat air fryer to 390°F.

2. Combine butter, salt and pepper in small bowl; mix well. Brush corn with butter mixture. Wrap each ear of corn in foil.*

3. Cook corn 6 to 8 minutes, turning halfway through cooking. Sprinkle with cheese, if desired.

*If your air fryer basket is too small to hold whole ears of corn, break them in half to fit.

DESSERTS

TOASTED POUND CAKE WITH BERRIES

makes 4 servings

1 package (10¾ ounces) frozen pound cake
2 tablespoons melted butter
1 cup fresh blackberries or blueberries

1 cup fresh raspberries or strawberries
Whipped topping, vanilla ice cream or prepared lemon curd (optional)

1 Cut pound cake into eight slices. Brush both sides of cake with butter.

2 Preheat air fryer to 370°F.

3 Cook cake slices in batches 5 to 7 minutes or until lightly browned, turning halfway through cooking.

4 Serve with berries and whipped topping, if desired.

HASSELBACK APPLES

makes 4 servings

2 medium apples
2 tablespoons packed brown sugar
2 tablespoons finely chopped walnuts

½ teaspoon ground cinnamon
2 tablespoons butter, melted
Vanilla ice cream (optional)

1 Cut apples in half vertically through stem. Scoop out and discard core and seeds.

2 Place apple halves flat sides down on cutting board; cut slices ⅛ inch apart almost all the way through. Place apples on sheet of foil; bring sides of foil up around apples, leaving top open.

3 Combine brown sugar, walnuts and cinnamon in small bowl; mix well. Brush butter over apples, letting butter drip between slices. Sprinkle with brown sugar mixture.

4 Preheat air fryer to 350°F. Place foil with apples in basket.

5 Cook apples 12 to 15 minutes or until softened and browned. Serve with ice cream, if desired.

NOTE: If apples brown too quickly on top, brush with additional melted butter.

TROPICAL PINEAPPLE RINGS

makes 10 servings

1 can (20 ounces) pineapple slices
    in pineapple juice
1 teaspoon coconut extract
2 eggs
½ cup all-purpose flour

1 cup unsweetened shredded
    coconut
1 cup panko bread crumbs
    Maraschino cherries (optional)

1 Drain pineapple slices, reserving juice. Place pineapple in large bowl; stir in ¼ cup reserved pineapple juice and coconut extract. Let stand at least 15 minutes.

2 Whisk eggs and remaining ½ cup pineapple juice in medium bowl until blended. Place flour in shallow dish. Combine coconut and panko in another shallow dish.

3 Drain pineapple; pat dry with paper towels. Coat pineapple with flour. Dip in egg mixture, letting excess drip back into bowl, then coat with coconut mixture. Place pineapple on baking sheet; refrigerate 15 minutes.

4 Preheat air fryer to 350°F. Spray basket with nonstick cooking spray.

5 Cook pineapple in batches 5 to 6 minutes or until coating is lightly browned and crisp, turning halfway through cooking. Serve warm; garnish with maraschino cherries.

CHOCOLATE–ORANGE LAVA CAKES

makes 4 servings

½ cup semisweet chocolate chips
¼ cup (½ stick) butter
½ cup powdered sugar, plus
  additional for garnish
2 eggs

2 egg yolks
½ teaspoon orange extract
3 tablespoons all-purpose flour
  Candied or grated orange peel
  (optional)

1 Combine chocolate chips and butter in microwavable bowl. Microwave on HIGH 45 seconds; stir until smooth.

2 Whisk in ½ cup powdered sugar, eggs, egg yolks and orange extract until blended. Add flour; stir just until blended.

3 Preheat air fryer to 370°F. Spray four 4-ounce ramekins with nonstick cooking spray. Pour batter into prepared ramekins.

4 Cook 10 to 12 minutes or until set. Remove ramekins to wire rack; cool 15 minutes.

5 Run knife around edges of cakes to loosen. Invert cakes onto plates; invert again onto serving plates. Sprinkle with additional powdered sugar; garnish with orange peel.

CINNAMON–SUGAR TWISTS >>

makes 14 twists

½ cup coarse sugar
1 teaspoon ground cinnamon

1 package (8 ounces) refrigerated crescent roll dough sheet

1. Combine sugar and cinnamon in shallow dish; mix well.

2. Unroll dough on cutting board or work surface; cut crosswise into 1-inch strips. Roll strips into thin ropes; fold ropes in half and twist halves together.

3. Preheat air fryer to 370°F. Spray basket with nonstick cooking spray.

4. Cook twists in batches 6 to 8 minutes or until golden brown, shaking halfway through cooking. Spray with cooking spray; roll in cinnamon-sugar to coat. Serve warm.

BLUEBERRY MUFFIN BREAD PUDDING

makes 4 servings

1½ cups milk
2 eggs
4 packages (2 ounces each) mini blueberry muffins, cut into 1-inch pieces

Powdered sugar or whipped topping (optional)

1. Spray four 6-ounce ramekins with nonstick cooking spray.

2. Whisk milk and eggs in medium bowl until blended. Add muffin pieces; stir to coat. Let stand 10 to 15 minutes to allow muffins to absorb milk mixture. Divide among prepared ramekins.

3. Preheat air fryer to 330°F.

4. Cook 8 to 10 minutes or until lightly browned. Sprinkle with powdered sugar, if desired.

BLOOMIN' BAKED APPLES

makes 2 servings

2 medium apples
2 tablespoons butter, melted
1 tablespoon granulated sugar
1 tablespoon packed brown sugar

½ teaspoon ground cinnamon
Vanilla ice cream (optional)
Caramel sauce, warmed (optional)

1. Cut ½-inch slice from tops of apples. Use paring knife or apple slicer to cut about eight lengthwise slices, being careful not to cut all the way through to bottom. Remove and discard apple cores and seeds.

2. Combine butter, granulated sugar, brown sugar and cinnamon in small bowl; mix well. Place apples in small baking dish that fits inside air fryer. Brush apples with butter mixture, letting mixture drip down into cuts between slices.

3. Preheat air fryer to 370°F.

4. Cook apples 15 to 20 minutes or until softened and lightly browned. Serve warm with ice cream; drizzle with caramel sauce, if desired.

DOUGHNUT HOLE FONDUE

makes 5 servings

1 package (about 6 ounces)
   refrigerated biscuit dough
   (5 biscuits)
3 tablespoons butter, divided
1 tablespoon sugar
¼ teaspoon ground cinnamon
¾ cup whipping cream

1 cup bittersweet or semisweet
   chocolate chips
½ teaspoon vanilla
   Sliced fresh fruit, such as
    pineapple, strawberries
    and cantaloupe

1 Separate dough into five pieces. Cut each piece in half; roll dough into balls to create 10 balls.

2 Place 2 tablespoons butter in small microwavable bowl; microwave on HIGH 30 seconds or until melted. Combine sugar and cinnamon in small dish; mix well. Dip balls in melted butter; roll in cinnamon-sugar to coat.

3 Preheat air fryer to 370°F. Spray basket with nonstick cooking spray.

4 Cook doughnut holes in batches 4 to 5 minutes or until golden brown.

5 Meanwhile, heat cream in small saucepan until bubbles form around edge. Remove from heat. Add chocolate chips; let stand 2 minutes or until softened. Add remaining 1 tablespoon butter and vanilla; whisk until smooth. Serve warm with doughnut holes and fruit for dipping.

CHOCOLATE–PEANUT BUTTER DESSERT WONTONS

makes 2 dozen wontons

24 wonton wrappers
½ cup peanut butter
½ cup chocolate hazelnut spread

Water
¼ cup chocolate sauce, warmed
Powdered sugar

1 Place wonton wrappers on work surface. Spoon about ½ teaspoon peanut butter and ½ teaspoon hazelnut spread in center of each wrapper.

2 Wet finger with water and spread around edges of wrapper. Fold squares into triangles; press edges to seal.

3 Preheat air fryer to 370°F.

4 Cook wontons in batches 4 to 5 minutes or until lightly browned. Transfer to serving plate.

5 Drizzle wontons with chocolate sauce; sprinkle with powdered sugar. Serve warm.

FRIED PINEAPPLE WITH TOASTED COCONUT

makes 8 servings

1 large pineapple, cored and
  cut into chunks
½ cup packed brown sugar
1 teaspoon ground cinnamon
½ teaspoon ground nutmeg
½ cup toasted coconut*
  Ice cream or whipped cream
  (optional)

Chopped macadamia nuts
  (optional)
Maraschino cherries (optional)

To toast coconut in air fryer, place coconut in ramekin. Cook in preheated 350°F air fryer 2 to 3 minutes or until lightly browned.

1 Place pineapple in large bowl. Combine brown sugar, cinnamon and nutmeg in small bowl; mix well. Sprinkle over pineapple; toss to coat. Refrigerate 30 minutes.

2 Preheat air fryer to 370°F. Spray basket with nonstick cooking spray.

3 Cook pineapple in batches 6 to 8 minutes or until browned and slightly crisp, shaking halfway through cooking.

4 Sprinkle with coconut. Serve with ice cream, if desired; garnish with nuts and cherries.

GOOEY DOUBLE CHOCOLATE BROWNIES

makes 8 servings

½ cup (1 stick) butter, melted
¾ cup unsweetened cocoa powder
1 cup sugar
2 eggs
⅔ cup all-purpose flour

½ teaspoon salt
½ cup semisweet chocolate chunks
　 or chips
Vanilla ice cream (optional)

1. Spray 7-inch cake pan* with nonstick cooking spray. Line bottom of pan with parchment paper; spray with cooking spray.

2. Place butter in medium microwavable bowl; microwave until melted. Stir in cocoa until well blended.

3. Preheat air fryer to 310°F.

4. Beat sugar and eggs in large bowl until well blended. Add cocoa mixture; stir until smooth. Add flour and salt; stir until blended. Stir in chocolate chunks. Spread batter in prepared pan; smooth top. Cover with foil.

5. Cook 45 minutes. Uncover; cook 10 minutes or until toothpick inserted into center comes out with fudgy crumbs. Cool on wire rack 15 minutes. Serve warm or at room temperature with ice cream, if desired.

If a 7-inch cake pan won't fit in your air fryer, a 6-inch cake pan may be used. Baking time will be slightly longer.

APPLE FRIES WITH CARAMEL SAUCE

makes 6 servings

APPLE FRIES

- ½ cup all-purpose flour
- 2 eggs
- 1 cup graham cracker crumbs
  or 4 large graham crackers, finely crushed
- ¼ cup granulated sugar
- 2 medium Gala apples, cut into 8 wedges each

CARAMEL SAUCE

- ½ cup packed brown sugar
- ¼ cup whipping cream
- 2 tablespoons butter
- 2 tablespoons light corn syrup
- ¼ teaspoon salt

1 Place flour in shallow dish. Beat eggs in another shallow dish. Combine graham cracker crumbs and granulated sugar in third shallow dish.

2 Coat apple wedges with flour. Dip in eggs, letting excess drip back into bowl, then coat with graham cracker crumb mixture. Place apples on plate; refrigerate 15 to 30 minutes.

3 Preheat air fryer to 390°F. Line basket with parchment paper.

4 Cook apples 6 to 8 minutes until slightly tender and golden brown.

5 Meanwhile, for sauce, combine brown sugar, cream, butter, corn syrup and salt in small saucepan; cook and stir over medium-low heat until well blended and heated through. Serve with apples.

METRIC CONVERSION CHART

VOLUME MEASUREMENTS (dry)

$1/8$ teaspoon = 0.5 mL
$1/4$ teaspoon = 1 mL
$1/2$ teaspoon = 2 mL
$3/4$ teaspoon = 4 mL
1 teaspoon = 5 mL
1 tablespoon = 15 mL
2 tablespoons = 30 mL
$1/4$ cup = 60 mL
$1/3$ cup = 75 mL
$1/2$ cup = 125 mL
$2/3$ cup = 150 mL
$3/4$ cup = 175 mL
1 cup = 250 mL
2 cups = 1 pint = 500 mL
3 cups = 750 mL
4 cups = 1 quart = 1 L

VOLUME MEASUREMENTS (fluid)

1 fluid ounce (2 tablespoons) = 30 mL
4 fluid ounces ($1/2$ cup) = 125 mL
8 fluid ounces (1 cup) = 250 mL
12 fluid ounces ($1 1/2$ cups) = 375 mL
16 fluid ounces (2 cups) = 500 mL

WEIGHTS (mass)

$1/2$ ounce = 15 g
1 ounce = 30 g
3 ounces = 90 g
4 ounces = 120 g
8 ounces = 225 g
10 ounces = 285 g
12 ounces = 360 g
16 ounces = 1 pound = 450 g

DIMENSIONS

$1/16$ inch = 2 mm
$1/8$ inch = 3 mm
$1/4$ inch = 6 mm
$1/2$ inch = 1.5 cm
$3/4$ inch = 2 cm
1 inch = 2.5 cm

OVEN TEMPERATURES

250°F = 120°C
275°F = 140°C
300°F = 150°C
325°F = 160°C
350°F = 180°C
375°F = 190°C
400°F = 200°C
425°F = 220°C
450°F = 230°C

BAKING PAN SIZES

Utensil	Size in Inches/Quarts	Metric Volume	Size in Centimeters
Baking or Cake Pan (square or rectangular)	8×8×2	2 L	20×20×5
	9×9×2	2.5 L	23×23×5
	12×8×2	3 L	30×20×5
	13×9×2	3.5 L	33×23×5
Loaf Pan	8×4×3	1.5 L	20×10×7
	9×5×3	2 L	23×13×7
Round Layer Cake Pan	8×1½	1.2 L	20×4
	9×1½	1.5 L	23×4
Pie Plate	8×1¼	750 mL	20×3
	9×1¼	1 L	23×3
Baking Dish or Casserole	1 quart	1 L	—
	1½ quart	1.5 L	—
	2 quart	2 L	—